A Sh

Anonymous

Stage 3

DORLION
Yayınları

A Shoemaker
Anonymous

İstiklal Mah. Yeşiltepe Sok.
24/A Eskişehir
Sertifika No: 33967

Editör: Aydın Sarıkaya

Çizimler: Gül Akyol

Kapak Tasarımı: İlker Şentürklü

ISBN: 978-605-249-069-3

Baskı-Cilt:
Bil Ofset
Tesviyeci Caddesi No:7/5 İskitler-Ankara
Sertifika No: 23261

dorlionyayinlari@gmail.com

dorlionyayinlari dorlionyayinlari

dorlionyayin

CONTENTS

Something About The War

"Will you tell me a story this evening, father?" asked William P. a fine lad of twelve years of age, the son of General P. who had been a gallant officer in the revolutionary war.

"And what story shall I tell you, my son?" said the general.

"Something about the war, father."

"You are always for hearing about the war, William," said General P: "I have told you almost all the stories I recollect. And besides, William, if you love to hear about war so well, when you are young, you will wish to be a soldier, when you become a man."

"And would you not wish to have me a soldier, father, if war should come? You were once a soldier, and I have heard people say, that you were very brave, and fought like a hero!"

"Well, well, William," said the general, "I must tell you one story more. Where are Henry and John? You may call them. They will like to hear the story too."

William, Henry and John enter.

Henry: "Father! William says you are going to tell us a story about the war! What-"

John: "Shall you tell us about some battle, where you fought?"

Gen. P: "Sit down, my children, sit down. Did I ever tell you about Enoch Crosby?"

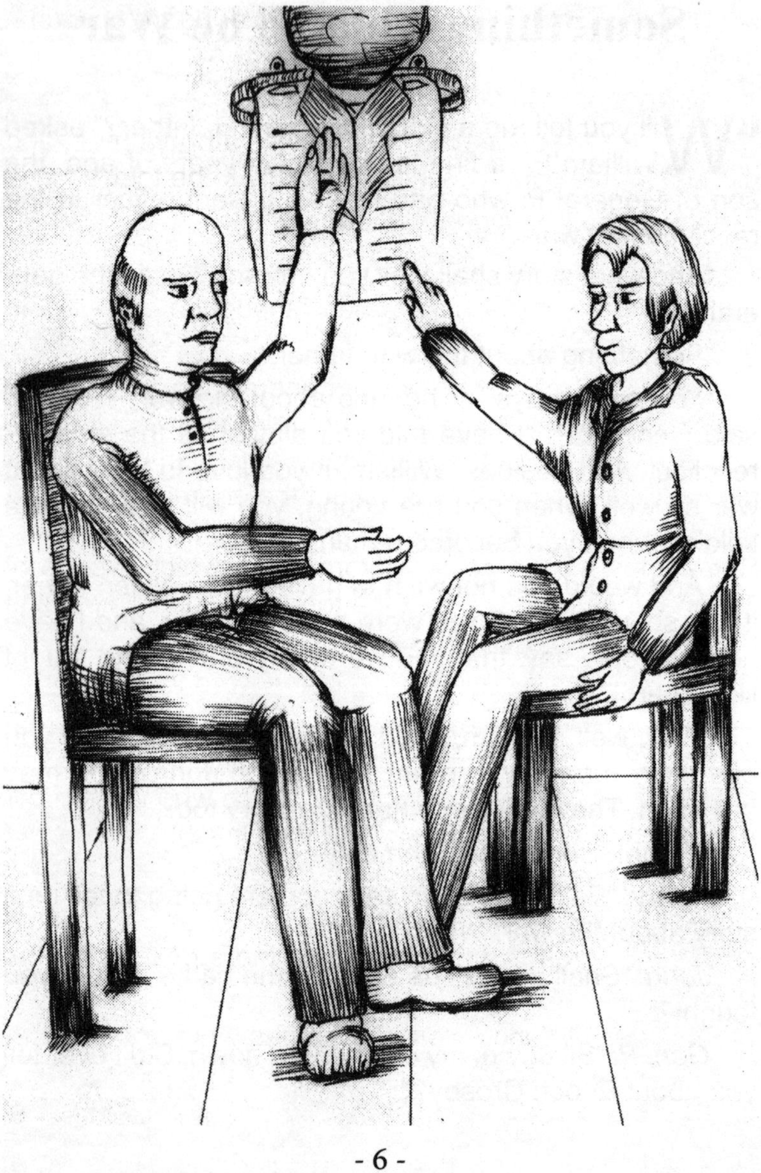

William: "Enoch Crosby? why, I never heard of such a man."

Henry: "Nor did I."

Gen. P: "I suppose not. But he was a brave man, and did that for his country, which is worthy to be told."

John: "Was he a general, father?"

Gen. P: "No. He was a spy."

William: "A spy! a spy! father, I thought a spy was an odious character?"

Gen. P: "Well, a real spy is generally so considered. I think it would be more appropriate to say, that he was an informer. During the war, many Americans were employed to obtain information about the enemy. They were often soldiers. They received pay, as did the soldiers. Sometimes they obtained information, which was very important, especially about the tories, or such Americans as favoured the British cause."

Henry: "Is that the meaning of the word tory?"

Gen. P: "Yes. Tories were Americans, who wished that the British aims might succeed, and the king of England might still be king of the colonies. Those who wished differently, and who fought against the British, were called whigs."

John: "Was Crosby a whig?"

Gen. P: "Yes. No man could be more devoted to the liberty of his country."

William: "Whence were the names whig and tory derived?"

Gen. P: "Do you wish to know the original meaning of the words, my son?"

William: "Yes, sir."

Gen. P: "The word tory, the learned Webster says, was derived from the Irish, in which language it signifies a robber. Tor, in that language, means a bush. And hence tory, a robber, or bushman. Because robbers often secrete themselves in the bushes. The meaning of the word whig, I am unable to tell you. Its origin is uncertain. It was applied, as I told you, to those who fought for the liberty of America."

William: "If the word tory means a robber, it was very properly applied to those, who wished to rob the people of America of their rights. Don't you think so, father?"

Gen. P: "Exactly so, William. A very just remark."

John: "Father! I thought you was going to tell about Enoch Crosby?"

Gen. P: "True, master John, we will begin."

The Early Life Of Crosby

Gen. P: "Enoch Crosby was born in Massachusetts, in 1750. When he was only three years old, his father took him, and the rest of his family, into the state of New-York to live. He was a farmer, and had bought a farm in Southeast, a town which borders on the state of Connecticut.

"Southeast is a wild, rough, and romantic place. Its hills are high and steep. Several cataracts tumble over precipices, and fall upon the ear with deafening noise.

"Two rivers, called the Croton and the Mill river, wind through the place. Several large ponds enrich the scenery.

"In this rude, but yet delightful country, Enoch Crosby lived, till he was sixteen years old. He was a strong and active boy. He could climb the highest hills without fatigue, and walk on the brink of frightful precipices without fear. His playmates admired him for his courage. He always took the lead because they wished it. They loved him, because he was generous and noble. When Enoch was, sixteen years of age, misfortune came upon his father. The family had lived comfortably. They were prosperous farmers. But now, a blast came. I know not the cause. But it came, and they were poor.

"Enoch's father decided that his son must learn a trade. It was no hardship for him to work. This he had been accustomed to. In those times, people laboured harder than now-a-days. Industry was a virtue.

"Idleness a shame. And it was hard labour, and solid fare, that made the men of those times so much stronger, than those of the present generation.

"Enoch loved labour, and was willing to learn a trade. But it was hard parting with friends, when the day arrived, that he was to go from home. It was settled that he should be a shoemaker, and should learn the trade of a man in a neighbouring town.

"The morning, at length, came, when he was to go. His bundle of clothes was nicely put up by his mother. And his father added a few shillings to his pocket. And then came the blessing of his worthy parents, with their good advice, that he should behave well, and attend to the duties of his place.

"And, said his tender mother. A tear starting from her eye, which she wiped away with the corner of her lindsey-woolsey, while she spake 'your Bible, Enoch, you will find in your bundle. Don't forget that. And you must pray for us. My son '

"She could say no more, and Enoch could hear no more. Without even bidding them 'farewell'. For his heart was too full for that. He shouldered his little pack, and took his way down the lane, which led to the road he was to take.

"At a few rods distance, he stopped to take one more look of the old place, so dear to him. His mother was standing at the window. She had felt the full tenderness of a mother for him before. But his love of home. His pause. His gaze. His tears. Now almost overwhelmed her.

"Enoch caught a glimpse of his mother, and saw her

agony. He could trust himself no longer, and summoning his energies, hurried over the hills, which soon hid the scenes of his youth from his view.

"In after years. Many years after. Even when he became an old man, he would speak of this scene, with deep feeling. He could never forget it. He said he felt for a time alone in the world. Cut off from all he held dear. I do not wonder," said *Gen. P:* "that he felt much, for well do I remember the pain I felt, the first time leaving home."

As A Soldier

G*en. P:* "Before night, Enoch reached his new home. His countenance had somewhat brightened. Yet his heart felt sad, for some days.

"On the following morning, his master introduced him into the shop. He had a seat assigned him provided with awls, thread, wax, and the more solid, but equally needful companion, a lapstone.

"Enoch proved a good apprentice. At first, the confinement was irksome. He had been used to the open air. To the active exercise of the field. To the free, healthful breeze of the mountain. It was tiresome to sit all day, in a confined shop. But he made himself contented, and, in a little time, found his employment quite pleasant."

John: "Didn't he want to see his mother?"

Gen. P: "Doubtless he did. He would not be likely to forget her. And I hope he did not neglect her good advice. And, when permission was given him, he went home to visit his friends, and always with delight.

"In 1771, the apprenticeship of Enoch ended. He was now twenty-one years old. A man grown. Industrious. Honest, and ready to begin business for himself.

"Old Mr. Crosby was a strong whig. A man of reading and information. One who took a deep interest in the welfare of his country.

"About the time that Enoch first left home to learn his trade, the troubles of America began with England. The king and his ministers became jealous of the Americans.

They thought them growing too fast 'They will soon,' said they, 'become proud, and wish to be free and independent. We must tax them. We must take away their money. This will keep them poor and humble.'

"Those things used often to be talked over, at old Mr. Crosby's. The neighbours would sometimes happen in there of a winter's evening to spend an hour, or two. The minister. The schoolmaster, and others. And although Southeast was a retired place, the conduct of the 'mother country,' as England was called, was pretty well understood there, and justly censured.

"Old Mr. Crosby, especially, condemned the conduct of England. He said, for one, he did not wish to be trampled on. 'They have no right to tax us,' said he. 'It is unjust. It is cruel, and, for myself, I am ready to say, I will not submit to it, and mark my word. The time will come, when the people will defend themselves. When that time comes, I hope,' said he. Looking round upon his sons, especially upon Enoch 'I hope my boys will not shame their father. No, not they.'

"Enoch thought much of his father. He was a grave man. One who sat steady in his chair when he talked. And he talked so slowly, and so emphatic, as always to be heard. Enoch, though a boy, listened. He was then interested. And as he grew older and was at home occasionally, on a visit, and these subjects were discussed.

He took a still deeper interest, and would sometimes even mingle in the animated talk, round the fire side of his father.

"And, then, there were times, too, when he was seated

on his bench. He was thinking over what he had heard. Or sat listening to some customer of his master, who happened in, on a rainy day. And who had seen the last paper which gave an account of some new attempt to oppress the colonies. At such times, he would almost wish himself a soldier, and in the field fighting for his country. And then the hammer, it was observed, would come down upon his lapstone with double force. As if he were splitting the head of one of the enemy open, or his awl would go through the leather, as if he were plunging a bayonet into the belt of a soldier."

"Such were the workings of Enoch Crosby's mind. The work of preparation was going on there. The steam was gradually rising. And though he realized it not. He was fitting to become a zealous and active soldier, in his country's service.

"On the 5th of March, 1770, nearly a year before Enoch's time was out, the 'Boston Massacre' happened."

Henry: "The 'Boston Massacre!' father. Pray, what was that?"

Gen. P: "William! you know the story, I trust. Can you tell it to your brother?"

William: "I have read about it. But I don't know well how to tell it. Will you tell it, father?"

Gen. P: "Tell it as well as you are able, my son. It is by practice that we learn to do things well."

William: "One evening some British soldiers were near a ropewalk in Boston. A man, who worked in the ropewalk, said something to them which they did not like, and they beat him.

"Three days after, on the 5th of March, while the soldiers were under arms, some of them were insulted by the citizens, and one, it is said, was struck. This soldier was so angry, that he fired. Then, six others fired. Three citizens were killed, and five were wounded.

"All Boston was soon roused. The bells were rung. Many thousand people assembled. They said that they would tear the soldiers to pieces, and I don't know but that they would have done so, if Gov. Hutchinson had not come out, and told the people. He would inquire into the matter, and have the guilty punished. This pacified them."

Gen. P: "Well done. Quite well done, master William. You now know, Henry, what is meant by the 'Boston Massacre.'"

Henry: "It was a bloody affair, I think."

Gen. P: "Bloody indeed!. Inhuman and highly provoking. The news of it spread. Spread rapidly, in every direction. The country was filled with alarm. War was seen to be almost certain. Such an insult. Such a crime could not be forgotten. Even at Phillipstown, where Crosby was at his trade, the story was told. It roused his spirit. He thought of what his father had said.

And he was even now desirous to enlist as a soldier, to avenge the slaughtered Americans.

"The next year. In January, I think it was. Enoch's time being out, he left his master, and went to live at Danbury, Connecticut, where he worked at his trade, as a journeyman, and here he continued for several years.

"During this time, the difficulties between England and America increased. The king and his ministers grew more haughty and oppressive. The Americans waxed more firm and confident. Several events tended to make the breach wider and wider. The British parliament taxed the Americans. Next the people of Boston threw into the sea a large quantity of tea, belonging to people in England, because a tax was laid upon it. Then, by way of revenge for this, the parliament ordered that no vessel should enter Boston harbour, or leave it. And, finally, the king sent a large body of English soldiers to America, to watch the people here, and force them to submission.

"Things now became quite unsettled. The Americans felt injured. They were provoked. Nothing was before them but war or slavery. This latter they could not bear. They scorned to be slaves. Besides, they saw no reason why they should be slaves. They knew war was a great evil. But it was better than slavery. And now they began to talk about it, and to act in view of it. In almost every town. Especially in New England. The young men were enrolled. That is, they were formed into companies, and were daily exercised, in order to make them good soldiers. These were called 'minute men'."

Henry: "Why were they called 'minute men,' father?"

Gen. P: "Because they stood ready to march at a minutes warning, should occasion require."

John: "Was Enoch Crosby a minute man?"

Gen. P: "No. He was not. But he stood ready to enlist, at any time when his services were needed.

"We will now pass on to the year 1775. In April of that year occurred the famous battle of Lexington. A party of British troops had been sent from Boston, to destroy some military stores, belonging to the Americans, at Concord, north of Boston.

On their way thither, they came to Lexington. And here they fired upon a small company of Americans, and killed several.

"It was a cruel act. Worthy only of savages. But it roused the Americans in that part of the country. And they immediately sent expresses. That is, men on horseback. To carry the tidings abroad.

"One of these expresses was directed to take his course for Danbury, and to speed his flight. On his arrival, he told the story.

"It produced alarm, and well it might. But it also produced resolution. The bells were rung. Cannon were fired. Drums beat to arms. Within a few hours, many people had assembled. The young and the old. All eager to do something for their country. One hundred and fifty young men came forward, and entered their names as soldiers.

"Chose a captain Benedict to lead them, and begged that they might go forth to the war. Enoch Crosby was the first man that entered his name on this occasion.

"Not long after, the regiment to which Crosby belonged marched to the city of New-York. Here they were joined by other companies, and sailed up Hudson's river to assist in taking Canada from the British.

"A short time before this, Ticonderoga, a fortress on lake Champlain, had been surprised by Col. Ethan Allen and his troops, and to them it had surrendered. This was an important post. Great rejoicings took place among the Americans, when it was known that this fort had fallen into their hands.

"The troop to which Crosby was attached, passed this fort, and proceeded to St. Johns, a British fort 115 miles north of Ticonderoga.

"This fort it was determined to attack. The troops were therefore landed, and preparations were made. Their number was one thousand. All young men,. Brave. Ardent. Resolute.

"Being formed in order of battle, the intrepid officers led them to the attack. As they advanced, the guns of the fort poured in upon them a tremendous fire. This they met manfully, and, though some fell, the others seemed the more determined.

But, just as they were beginning the attack in good earnest, a concealed body of Indians rose upon them, and the appalling war whoop broke upon their ears."

"This savage yell they had never before heard. Such a sight they had never before witnessed. For a moment, alarm spread through the ranks, but courage. Action was now necessary. Death or victory was before them. The officers called them to rally, to stand their ground, and they did so. They opened a well directed fire upon their savage foes, and only a short time passed before the latter were glad to retreat.

"The savages having retired, the men were ordered to throw up a breast work, near the place, to shelter themselves from the guns of the fort. This was done expeditiously. Trees were felled, and drawn to the spot by some, while others were employed in throwing up earth.

"During these labours of the Americans, the enemy continued to annoy them, by throwing shells from the fort."

William: "Pray, father, what are shells? I have read of them. But I do not know more than that they are a kind of shot."

Gen. P: "Shells are often called bombs, a word which signifies great noise. Because, when they burst, they make a great noise. They consist of a large shell of cast iron, which is round and hollow. A hole is made through the shell to receive a fusee, as it is called. This is a small pipe, or hollow piece of wood, which is filled with some combustible matter. When a bomb is about to be fired, it is filled with powder, after which the fusee is driven into the vent, or hole of the shell."

William: "How are bombs fired, father?"

Gen. P: "They are thrown from a kind of cannon called a mortar. It has its name from its resemblance to a common mortar. The lower part of the mortar is called the chamber, which contains the powder. When fired, the powder in the chamber not only sends the bomb. But at the same time, it sets fire to the fusee, which continues to burn slowly, as it passes through the air. The calculation always is, to have the fire from the fusee reach the powder in the shell. At the moment the latter reaches the ground. It then bursts, and the scattering fragments of iron often do horrible execution."

William: "Did you say, father, that mortars were short guns?"

Gen. P: "Land mortars are quite short. Sea mortars, or such as are used on board vessels, are longer and heavier, because they are usually fired at greater distances. A land mortar, which will throw a shell thirteen inches in diameter, weighs thirteen hundred weight. The weight of the shell is about one hundred and seventy-five pounds. It contains between nine and ten pounds of powder and is fired by means of about the same quantity of powder."

William: "Pray, father, who invented bombs?"

Gen. P: "The inventor is not known. They have been in use since the year 1634. Some years after the above affair, Crosby himself related the manner in which the soldiers contrived to escape unhurt. When a shell rose in the air, every one would stop working, and watch its course, to ascertain whether it would fall near him. If it appeared to approach so near, as to endanger any one, he would dodge behind something, till it had burst, or passed by."

John: "Father, could a soldier dodge a cannon ball?"

Henry: "Why, John! I should think you knew enough, not to ask so foolish a question."

Gen. P: "Not so bad a question neither, master Henry. Under some circumstances, a cannon ball might he avoided."

William: "Not when it is first fired, father."

Gen. P: "True. But when it has nearly spent its force, a person might easily get out of its way. But even when a ball only rolls along the ground, apparently slow, it would be dangerous to attempt to stop it: especially if large. I recollect to have read of a soldier, who saw a ball rolling towards him, which he thought to stop with his foot. But, poor fellow! it broke his leg in an instant.

"Some of the American soldiers at St. Johns, were too intent upon their labour, to pay much attention to the shells. Crosby was one. All on a sudden, a fellow-soldier near by called out in a tone of thunder, 'Crosby! look out! take care! take care!' Crosby looked up, and directly over him, a shell was descending."

"He had but a minute to think. He dropped flat upon the ground, and the shell just passed over him. 'A miss,' thought he, 'is as good as a mile', but he said, after such a warning, he kept one eye upon the enemy.The rude fortification was soon completed, and served as a shelter till night, when the American troops silently departed. Taking to their boats, the next day they reached the Isle Aux Noix?"

William: "Is not that a French name?"

Gen. P: "Yes. My son. A name given to the Island, while the French had possession of it. Do you know where it lies?"

William: "It is a small island, near the northern extremity of Lake Champlain."

Gen. P: "Right. It is pronounced Eel-o-nwar, and signifies the island of nuts."

John, "Did the people find walnuts there, father?"

Gen. P: "Some kind of nuts doubtless, my son. But whether walnuts, or hazel nuts, or some other kind, I am unable to say."

Henry: "Pray, John, don't ask so many foolish questions, I want to hear the story."

Gen. P: "But you would wish your brother to know the reason of things, would you not, master Henry? It was quite a proper question, and one it seems none of us can answer. We must examine the point some time, and let master John know.

"The American troops had not been long a this island, before many of them were taken sick and sent to the hospital. Crosby was of the number. But he had no idea of confinement. In a few days, he resolved to join the army again. To this the surgeon remonstrated. It might be his death he said. But the valiant soldier could not be persuaded, and again appeared at camp.

"'What!' exclaimed Capt. Benedict, when he saw him, 'have you got back, Crosby? I never expected to see you again. You look too ill to be here. You would make a better scare-crow than soldier, I fancy, just now.'

"'Well, captain! said Crosby, 'if I'm a scare-crow, I can frighten the enemy, if I cannot fight them. So I shall be of some service."'

John: "Well, father, did they hang up Crosby for a scare-crow?"

Henry: "Why, you simpleton, John, don't you know better?"

Gen. P: "Crosby was quite ill. But his resolution made him forget how feeble he was. He was a scare-crow to the enemy in a different way from that which Capt. Benedict meant. A battle soon came on, and before night Enoch Crosby was marching into the enemy's fort to the tune of Yankee Doodle, to assist in taking care of the prisoners."

John: "But, I thought he was too ill to fight."

Gen. P: "A soldier, at such a time, and such a soldier as Crosby, would be likely to forget his weakness. He went bravely through the day. And from that time rapidly regained his health.

"Success now followed the American troops, and in November, Montreal was taken.

"The time, for which Crosby had enlisted, had now expired, and he concluded to return home. Accordingly, he embarked with several others, in a small schooner, for Crown Point, twelve miles north of Ticonderoga. Thence they came by land to this latter place. From which they proceeded home ward for some distance by water, and then by land. Their rout lay through a wilderness. It was now winter, and the cold was intense. Provisions were scarce.

Comfortable lodgings were not to be found. Their prospects were often gloomy, and their distress indescribable.

"At length, however, they reached their respective homes. After a short stay with his friends, Crosby once more returned to Danbury, and again betook himself to the peaceful occupation of shoemaking."

Singular Adventures

G*en. P:* "Crosby was well contented, for a time, to pursue his occupation.

He had seen hard service, in the northern campaign, and needed rest.

"During the following summer, however, his patriotic feelings began again to stir within him. The war was going on, with redoubled fury. The British had, in several instances, gained the advantage. The Americans needed more soldiers, and it was thought that unless the friends of liberty came forward. Promptly came, the British arms might succeed.

"It was not in such a man as Enoch Crosby, to seek ease, or shun danger, in the hour of his country's trial. He saw others making sacrifices. Women as well as men. Youth as well age.

"And he scorned to have it said, that he could not make sacrifices, as well as others. His musket was therefore taken down, and fitting on his knapsack, he took up his march towards the head quarters of the American army on the Hudson. In a few days, he reached the neutral ground and.."

William: "Pray, father, may I interrupt you, to inquire what was meant by the 'neutral ground?"

Gen. P: "I will explain it to you. At this time (Sept. 1776,) the head quarters of the British army were in the city of New York. The American army lay up the Hudson, fifty or sixty miles, either at, or near, West Point.

"Between the two armies, therefore, was the county of West Chester, the centre of which being occupied by neither, was called the 'neutral ground.' But, in reality, it was far from being a neutral spot."

William: "Why not, father, if neither the British, nor the Americans, occupied it?"

Gen. P: "Because, my son, it was here that a great number of tories resided. The worst enemies which the Americans had to contend with."

Henry: "Worse than the British, father?"

Gen. P: "In several respects worse. The tories, in general, were quite as unfriendly to American liberty, as the British themselves. And, besides, living in the country, and being acquainted with it, they could do even more injury than strangers.

"Many of this description of persons lived on the 'neutral ground;' What was worse, they often pretended to be Whigs, passed for such, but in secret, did all in their power to injure their country.

"Crosby, as I told you, had reached a part of this ground, on his way to the American camp. It was just at evening, that he fell in with a stranger, who appeared to be passing in the same direction with himself.

"'Good evening,' said the stranger 'which way are you travelling? Below?'"

William: "Which way was that?"

Gen. P: "Towards New-York. The British were sometimes called the 'lower party'. The Americans the 'upper party' because the latter lay north of the former.

The stranger meant to ascertain which party Crosby was going to join."

Henry: "And did Crosby tell him?"

Gen. P: "No: he replied, that he was too much fatigued to go much farther that evening, either above or below. But he believed he should join himself to a bed, could he find one.

"'Well,' said the stranger, 'listen to me. It will soon be dark. Go with me. I live but a short distance from this. You shall be welcome.'

"Crosby thanked him, and said he would gladly accept his kind invitation.

"'Allow me to ask,' said the soldier, 'your advice, as to the part which a true friend of his country should take, in these times?'

"'Do I understand you?' inquired the stranger. His keen eye settling on the steady countenance of Crosby 'do you wish to know, which party a real patriot should join?'

"'I do,' said Crosby.

"'Well! you look like one to be trusted '

"'I hope I am honest,' replied Crosby.

"'Why,' observed the stranger, 'one mus'n't say much about oneself, in these days. But some of my neighbours would advise you to join the lower party.'

"'Why so?' asked Crosby.

"'Why, friend, they read, that we must submit to the powers that be. And, besides, they think king George is a good friend to America, notwithstanding all that is said against him.'

"'Could you introduce me to some of your neighbours of this way of thinking?' asked Crosby.

"'With all my heart,' replied the stranger, 'I understand they are about forming a company to go below, and I presume they would be glad to have you join them.'

"'I do not doubt it,' observed Crosby.

"'Well, friend,' said the stranger, 'say nothing. Rest yourself to night. And, in the morning, I will put you in the way to join our. The company.'

"By this time, they had reached the stranger's dwelling. It was a farm house, situated a short distance from the main road, and retired. But quite neat and comfortable in its appearance. Here the soldier was made welcome by the host and his family. After a refreshing supper, Crosby excused himself. He was soon asleep. And 'slept well."'

John: "Was that man a tory, father?"

Henry: "Why, John, you know he was. It is as clear as day."

Gen. P: "Yes, my son, he was a tory. In heart a firm tory. But he intended to be cautious. He intended to ascertain, if possible, which side Crosby favoured, before he expressed his own views. But, when Crosby asked to be introduced to some of his neighbours, he concluded that if urged, he would go below. And after this was more unreserved."

William: "Did Crosby tell him that he would go below?"

Gen. P: “No, no, he only asked to be introduced to some of the tories.”

Henry: “But did he not do wrong to conceal his opinions?”

Gen. P: “Certainly not. A person is not under obligation to tell all about his opinions, to every one. When a man speaks, he should indeed tell that which is true. But he is not bound, unless under certain circumstances, to tell the whole truth.

“Crosby, I said, slept well. In the morning, a better breakfast than usual graced the farmer’s table, and the keen appetite of the soldier, after a good night’s rest, did it honour.

“When breakfast was over, Crosby reminded his host of his last night’s promise to introduce him to some of his neighbours thereabouts. Particularly to those, who were about forming a company.

“‘True,’ said the farmer, ‘I will accompany you. They will welcome such a soldier-like looking lad as yourself. They like men of bone and muscle.’

“In a walk of a few miles, they saw quite a number of the friends of the royal cause. Crosby was introduced as one who was desirous of serving his country, and as willing to hear what could be said, in favour of joining their standard.

“They had much to say. Many arguments to support their way of thinking, and strongly did they urge Crosby to go with them. As he was introduced by the farmer, who was known to be a true tory, they talked without disguise.

They told their plans. Spoke of the company which was forming. And particularly of a meeting, which they were to hold a few nights from that time. And now, said they, 'come and join us.'

"Crosby told them that he should think of their proposition, and rather thought that he should contrive to pay them a visit at the appointed time.

"Little did they think, what sort of a visit the soldier was planning.

"In the course of a couple of days, Crosby had gained all the information he wished, and now determined to depart. He told the farmer, therefore, on the morning of the third day, that it was not worth while for him to wait longer. He had a strong wish to join the army, and believed that he should go along.

"The farmer said some things, by way of persuading Crosby to wait a day or two, when the company would meet, and then he could enlist and go with them.

"To this Crosby replied, that unexpected delays might occur, and he thought it would be better for him to proceed.

"'But,' said he, as he shook hands with the unsuspicious farmer, and bade him farewell, 'I shall doubtless have the pleasure of seeing the company;' and added, 'It is my intention to join them at -.'

"'Very well, very well!' interrupted the farmer,. His eye brightening at his success, in having, as he thought, made Crosby a convert to the royal cause. "'I hope it will be well'.

Whispered Crosby to himself, as he walked down the lane, which led to the road 'I will try to join them. But I may be in a manner not so agreeable to them.'

"On reaching the road, to avoid the mischief which might come upon him, if he went directly north. He took the road leading to New-York. But from this, soldier like, he soon filed off, crossing a thicket, shaped his course northerly towards the American camp.

"He was soon beyond harm, and now travelled at his ease. He had heard of a Mr. Young, who lived at a distance, in a direction somewhat different from that which he was taking. And as he was said to be a true whig, he concluded to repair to him, and to concert measures to take the company of tories, at the time of their meeting.

"With this resolution he again altered his course, so as to strike the road leading to Mr. Young's. Unexpected difficulties, however, impeded his course. Hills, woods, streams, and before he reached the house, it was near midnight.

"It so happened, fortunately, that Mr. Young was still up, although his family had all retired. A light was still burning, and Crosby made for the door, which led into the room where Mr. Young sat.

"He gave a gentle rap at the door, which was soon cautiously opened. Cautiously, because it was now late. And, in those times, no one knew when he was safe.

"The light fell on Crosby's face, and the searching eye of Mr. Young followed.

"'Sir,' said Crosby, in haste to make his excuse, 'I understand you are a true friend to your country, and I have important '

"'Come in, come in,' said Mr. Young. The expression of Crosby's face carrying more conviction of honesty, than words could do 'come in. You travel late '

"'I have reason for it,' replied the now animated soldier'

I am told you are a friend to the upper party. I have something to tell you which may be important."

"'What is it,' asked Mr. Young.

"'Sir,' said Crosby 'do you know the character of the people who live around you?'

"'I think I do,' said Mr. Young.

"'They are traitors,' said Crosby.

"'Many are. Too many,' said Mr. Young 'but they pass for friends, and it is difficult to discriminate. Difficult to bring them to justice.'

"'Well!' said Crosby, 'I have the means of pointing them out. I have been among them. I know them. I know their plans.'

"'Can you give me their names?' eagerly inquired Mr. Young. At the same time rising from his seat.

"'I can do more,' rejoined Crosby. And then he went on to relate the interviews which he had had. And about the contemplated meeting of the company, two nights following 'and,' said the soldier, 'if you will assist me, we will join them, as I promised, and make them march to the tune of good old 'yankee doodle,' instead of 'God save the king.'

"'With all my heart,' exclaimed Mr. Young. Taking down his hat 'no time is to be lost. The committee of safety are at White Plains. They must know it tonight.'"

William: "'The committee of safety!' father, who were they?"

Gen. P: "Your inquiry is well suggested. The committee of safety consisted of men of distinction friendly to the liberties of their country. They were appointed in almost every district throughout the land. It was their business to watch over the interest of the country in their vicinity, to obtain information, and, when necessary, to seize upon suspected persons."

William: "Who were the committee at White Plains?"

Gen. P: "The principal man was John Jay, who afterwards went ambassador to England.

"Mr. Young and Crosby were soon on their way to White Plains, which lay but a few miles distant. Crosby was not a little fatigued. But his zeal was now all alive, and made him quite forget his weariness.

"It was near two o'clock, before they reached the quarters of Mr. Jay. He was soon summoned, and listened with deep interest to the tale of Crosby. It was important intelligence. Precisely the information desired, he said. And he promised, at early dawn, to call the committee together, and consult what should be done.

"Mr. Young and Crosby now retired to a neighbouring

inn. But the door was fastened, and the landlord was fast locked in sleep. They rapped at the door, and called, and, as you say, Master Henry, when you speak Monsieur Tonson.

"'And loud indeed were they obliged to bawl,

Ere they could rouse the torpid lump of clay.'

"The door, however, was at length opened, and after receiving a growl from the landlord, and a snarl from the landlady, that their rest should be thus broken. They were shown to a bed room, where both in the same bed soon forgot the toils of the night, in a refreshing sleep.

"The committee were together at an early hour, as had been promised. Again Crosby told over his story. And when he had finished, 'Are you willing,' asked the committee, 'to accompany a body of horse to the spot, and attempt to take the traitors?'

"'Sure I am,' said Crosby. 'I gave them encouragement that I would 'join' them, and well should I like to fulfil such an engagement.'

"'You shall have an opportunity,' said the committee. 'Hold yourself in readiness, and may success crown the enterprise.'

"'At the appointed time, a company of troop well mounted, left White Plains. And, under the pilotage of Crosby, directed their course towards the spot. In the mean time, the company had assembled, and now, amid the darkness of the night, were arranging their plans - "

"'What noise is that!' asked one. Rising from his seat, and turning his ear towards the quarter whence the sound came. "'Nothing, I guess,' said a witty sort of fellow, in one corner of the room, 'but my old horse, taking lessons at the post, before - '

"'Something more serious, perhaps,' said the farmer, with whom Enoch Crosby had quartered, 'that yankee!'

"'Where is he?' asked a dark eyed, keen sighted tory, rising from his seat 'I didn't much like his looks, the other day.'

"'Something serious abroad!'. Exclaimed several at the same time rising 'Captain! Captain!'

"'Go to the door,' thundered the Captain of the gang 'and reconnoitre'

"'You are prisoners!' exclaimed a voice which struck a panic through the clan, as the door was opened 'surrender, or you are dead men!'

"'By whose authority is this?' asked the captain of the tories, rushing to the door, with his sword drawn, followed by his clan, with their guns uncharged.

"'We demand it in the name of the Continental Congress'. Exclaimed he of the whigs.

"'We surrender to nothing. But to superior strength,' said the tory captain. 'Soldiers! come on.'

"'My brave comrades! advance,' exclaimed the leader of the patriots 'death or victory. Make ready!'

"'It's of no use to contend,' said the farmer 'not a gun loaded, captain! we're betrayed! a blight on that yankee!'"

"'Take aim!'. Uttered the patriot leader.

"'Hold! hold!' exclaimed the captain of the tories 'it's needless to shed blood. What are your terms?'"

"'Immediate surrender!' replied the commander of the whigs.

"'Done'. Rejoined the leader of the traitors. And now they were marched out, and were tied together in pairs, and were conducted to prison, some miles distant to the tune, of 'Rogue's march.'"

William: "Was Crosby seen by them?"

Gen. P: "Probably not. The darkness of the night would conceal him. And it was needless to expose himself, as their betrayer. He was suspected by some. Especially by the farmer, who recollected a significant look which Crosby gave him, when he left him."

Henry: "He was justly rewarded, was'n't he, father?"

Gen. P: "Justly, indeed!. And all the rest, who were designing to sacrifice their country's liberty and honour."

As A Prisoner

G*en. P:* "Crosby felt quite satisfied with hissuccess. But not more so, than the committee of safety. They sent for him. Told him he had done his country real service, and wished to know what his plans were. "'You are going to enlist into the army, are you?' asked Mr. Jay.

"'I am,' replied Crosby. 'My country needs my services, and she shall have them.'

"'Your resolution is honourable,' said Mr. Jay 'but may you not be of greater service, in another way? We have enemies among us. Secret foes. Who are plotting our ruin. We need information respecting them. We wish for some one, who has prudence and skill. One, who will go round the country. Who will find out where these men live. Where they meet and form their plans. It is a dangerous service,. But, then, the reward.'

"'I care not for danger,' said Crosby 'my country is dear to me. My life is at her service. Sir, I will go. But one thing I ask, only one, if I fall, do justice to my memory. Let the world know, that Enoch Crosby was in your service. In the service of his country. And that he fell a martyr to the cause of liberty.'

"'It shall be done,' said Mr. Jay 'we pledge it, by our sacred honour.'

"'But,' continued he to Crosby, 'let no man know your secret. No, not even should you be taken. If you are ever taken by the Americans, as belonging to the British, we will help you to escape.

But, if you cannot let us know, here is a paper, which in the last extremity, you may show, and it will save you."'

William: "What did that paper contain?"

Gen. P: "It was what is called a pass. It was signed by the committee of safety. And ordered that the person who had it should be suffered to pass without injury.

"In a few days, Crosby was ready. He had provided himself with a peddlar's pack, in which he had put a set of shoemaker's tools. His design was to go round the country, and work at his trade. And, at the same time, to get such information as might be useful to his employers."

"Not long after he set out upon his adventures, he arrived just at evening at a small house, at which he knocked, hoping to procure a night's lodging.

"It was some time before he was heard. At length a girl came, and inquired his errand.

"'I wish for a lodging tonight,' said Crosby 'if it may be' "'I don't know, sir,' replied the girl 'I'll go and ask mother.'

"The girl soon reappeared, and bade him walk in. On reaching the kitchen, he made known his wishes, to the mistress of the family.

"'Lodgings! sir. Did you ask for lodgings? we don't keep lodgings here, sir.'

"'I suppose not, madam,' said Crosby, in a kind manner 'but I am quite fatigued, and thought, perhaps, you would let me stay till morning.'

"'I don't know but what you may. The man is gone from home. There's such work now-a-days, that a body don't know nothing what to say or do. Pray, what do you carry in that huge pack?'

"'In this pack, madam? only some shoemaker's tools. I am a shoemaker, madam. Perhaps, you have some work for me to do? I'll take it off with your leave.'

"'Well, do as you please. Our John wants a pair of shoes. And perhaps the man of the house will give you the job when he comes home.'

"'I shall be glad to do it,' said Crosby. 'Madam, have you heard the news?'

"'What news?'

"'Why, that Washington is on the retreat, and that the British army is pursuing him, and likely to overtake him.'

"'Ah! that's good news,' exclaimed the old lady, 'you may stay here tonight. Sally! Sally! here get this man some supper. He brings good news. I hope the rebels every one will be shot. Sally!. Make up the best bed. Here's a chair. Sit down, sir, make yourself at home.

"Crosby accordingly took a seat. Supper was soon ready, and he eat heartily.

"When he had done, he drew his chair to the fire, about which time, the man of the house came in. He was told the good news by his wife, and Crosby was made welcome.

"The evening was spent in talking about the war, and the prospects of the country. The host proved himself a firm tory, and wondered that Crosby and every one else should not think and feel precisely as he did.

"'Have you many of your way of thinking in these parts?' inquired Crosby.

"'That we have,' replied the host 'more than we shall have a few days hence.'

"'I hope so,' whispered Crosby to himself. 'But, sir, how so?' inquired he, with some surprise.

"'Why,' replied the host, 'you must know that we've a company nearly ready to march. I guess they'll go the sooner, now that the British are after Washington. They'll wish to get there in time to see some of the fun.'
"'Could you introduce me to some of the company?' asked Crosby.

"'That I can. You'd better join them. I'll tell you what. You'll have good pay and short work.'

"The following morning, after breakfast, the host took Crosby abroad, and introduced him to the captain of the tory company, as one who, perhaps, might be persuaded to enlist.

"'Would you like to enlist?' asked the captain. At the same time running his eye over the stout frame of Crosby.

"'I would like to see your muster-roll, first,' replied Crosby."

Henry: "Pray, father, what is a muster-roll?"

Gen. P: "A paper, my son, on which the names of the soldiers are registered."

Henry: "Why did Crosby wish to see that?"

Gen. P: "I was going to tell you. He wished to ascertain who had joined the company."

William: "Did the captain show him the roll?"

Gen. P: "Yes. And carefully did Crosby run over the names.

"'Will you join us?' asked the captain, when Crosby had finished looking at the roll.

"'They are all strangers to me,' said Crosby, 'and besides, I fear that the roll may fall into the hands of the Americans. Then, what will become of us?'

"'No fear of that,' said the captain. 'Come with me, and see how we manage.'

"Crosby was now led into a large meadow, at no great distance, in which stood a large stack of hay.

"'Look at this stack, sir. What do you think of this?'

"'It is monstrous,' said Crosby. 'Why so much hay in one stack?'

"'Not so much neither, replied the captain, 'it isn't every one that knows how to manage. Here, take a look inside,' at the same time drawing aside some long hay, which concealed an apartment within.

"Crosby started. The stack was hollow. Capable of holding at least fifty men."

"'Ha! ha! ha!' roared out the captain, 'you are afraid the muster roll will fall into bad hands. Are you?

"Well, what think you now? Is that likely, when we know how to manage?

Many a rebel has passed by this stack. But he hadn't

brains enough to think what was inside. Come, my good fellow, shall I enter your name?'

"'I'll think of it,' said Crosby, 'and let you know soon.'

"While Crosby was apparently making up his mind, the day passed by. He was still at the captain's, who invited him to spend the night. This invitation was accepted, and at an early hour, he retired to rest.

"But he could not sleep. What should he do?

"He thought. Pondered. Hesitated. But at length, resolved. Midnight came. He rose, and having put on his clothes, softly passed from his chamber down stairs.

"At every step he listened. All was still. Without disturbing even the wary captain, he left the premises, and was soon on his way towards White Plains.

"An hour or two brought him to the residence of Mr. Jay, whom he called from his bed, and to whom he related what he knew. A plan was soon concerted, by which to take the whole company. This being settled, Crosby hastened back. And, before any one was up at the captain's, was safely, and without having excited suspicion, in his bed.

"In the course of the day, he was strongly urged to enlist. But he wished to see the company together, he said. 'You shall see them together,' said the captain, 'it would be well to meet. We must arrange matters before we go.'

"A hasty summons, was therefore, sent round, and before nine o'clock that night, the whole company had assembled. It was a season of great joy among them. The rebels, they said, were so depressed, that they would have but little to do. But to march down and see them ground arms.

"'Well, Mr. Crosby,' bawled out the captain, 'what say you? will you go with us, and'

"'Hark! hark! hark!' exclaimed a soldier, who sat near the door 'I hear horses approaching.'

"'Out with the lights!. Out with the lights!' said the captain 'silence every man. Keep your places.'

"At this moment, a loud rap was heard at the door. Soon after which it was thrown open, and the word 'surrender,' uttered by an officer, came in like a peal of thunder.

"'Who are you?' demanded the tory captain, rising with some effort. His knees trembling under him.

"'Who am I!' uttered the same voice, 'you will soon know who I am, unless you surrender. You are surrounded. You are prisoners.'

"Dismay now filled the company. They rose, and in the darkness which pervaded the room, attempted to escape. In the haste and confusion, chairs were broken. Benches overturned. Pitchers and tumblers dashed in pieces. Some plunged from the windows, and were taken. Others felt their way up chamber, and hid in the garret, while several, in attempting to reach the cellar, were plunged headlong upon the bottom.

"In a little time, however, matters were more quiet. The horsemen had surrounded the house, and none could escape. From their hiding places they were, at length, dragged. Poor Crosby with the rest and tied together in pairs, were marched to the village of White Plains."

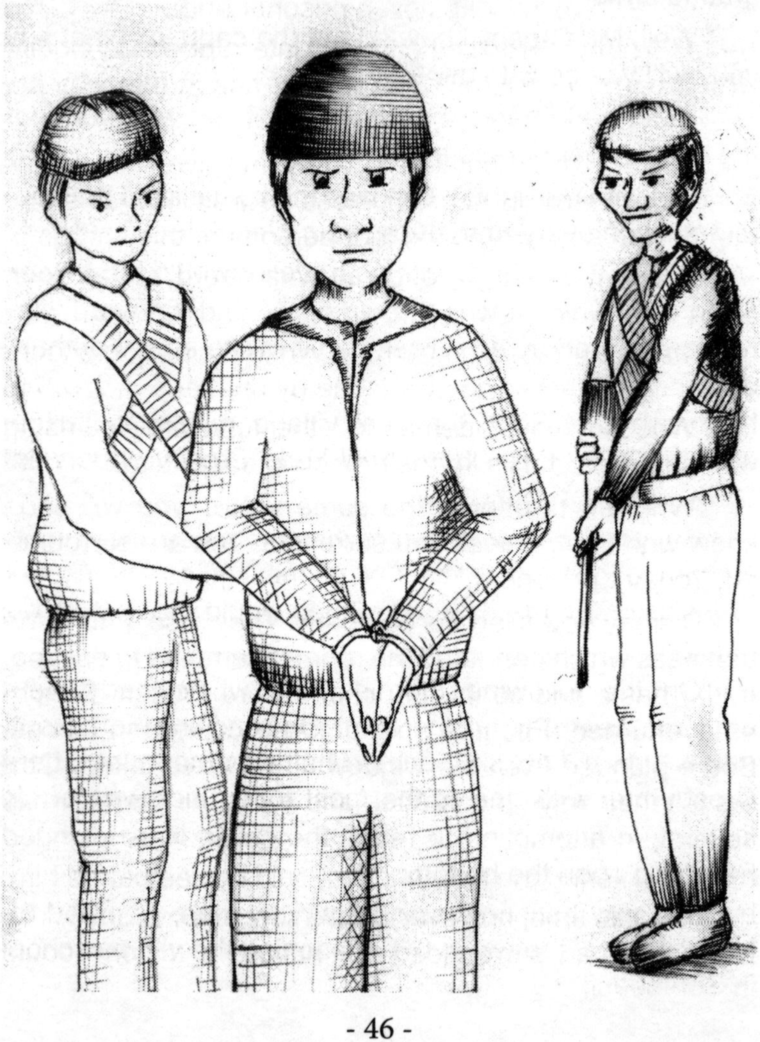

Crosby's Escape

G*en. P:* "Crosby was now a prisoner and..."

Henry: "Pray, father, may I interrupt you to inquire why Crosby did not tell who he was, and in that way escape?"

Gen. P: "The committee of safety had given him orders at no time to tell his secret, unless he was likely to suffer death. Had it been known, that persons of this character were abroad in the country, no traveller would have been safe.

"On the arrival of the party, at White Plains, the prisoners were examined privately, one by one, and ordered to be marched to Fishkill, a small village, near the Hudson, about seventy miles from New York. Crosby underwent an examination also.

"But when he came before the committee, they highly commended him. Told him that he must go as if a prisoner to Fishkill. But, in a little time, they would provide for his escape.

"On the following morning, the whole party were early on their way up the river. On reaching Fort Montgomery, near Peekskill, a short halt was made, and here Crosby met with one of the most trying incidents of his life.

"On entering the fort, whom should he see before him, but his former schoolmaster. A worthy man, who had often been at his father's, while teaching the village school in Southeast.

"And well did that schoolmaster know the attachment of old Mr. Crosby to American liberty. Yet, here was his son, among a set of tories and a prisoner.

"The schoolmaster started back, with a kind of horror, and even Crosby was for a moment nearly overcome.

"'Is this possible?' exclaimed the schoolmaster, 'do my eyes serve me? Enoch Crosby! Why do I see you thus?'

"Crosby advanced, and taking his old friend by the hand, replied, 'you see me just as I am. Among tories, and a prisoner. But I have no explanations to offer."

"'No explanations!' uttered the other 'are you, then, indeed, an enemy to your country? Oh! your poor old father, Enoch. It will bring down his gray hairs with sorrow to the grave when he hears of this.'

"For a moment, Crosby felt a faintness come over him. His father! he loved him. Revered him. But he could not explain. It would not do. He, therefore, only replied, that God was his judge, and the time might come, when things would appear otherwise than they did. In the midst of this conversation. Painful and unsatisfactory to both, the drum sounded 'the roll,' and Crosby had time only to press the hand of his old friend, which he did with affection. He was soon on his way. Sadly depressed for a time, lest his father should hear his story, without the appropriate explanation. But he comforted himself that he was doing his duty to his country.

"And, perhaps, thought he, a few months may give us

the victory, and then my father and friends will know all, and will love me the better for the part I am acting.

"The party at length reached Fishkill, and were conducted to an old Dutch church, where they were confined and strictly watched.

"Within a few days, the committee of safety arrived in the village, to examine the prisoners more strictly. Crosby, in his turn, was summoned to appear. But in respect to him, the committee only consulted how he might escape.

"There were difficulties in every plan they could think of. There was danger. Great danger. Yet they could not appear to favour him. And their advice to him was, to run the hazard of an attempt by night, in the best way he could contrive. And should he be so fortunate as to escape, he might find a safe retreat with a Mr. - , who lived at some distance.

"Crosby, at length, thought of a plan. Near the northwest corner of the church was a window, from which he contrived to draw the fastenings, so that he could open it. Near this window, stood a large willow tree, whose deep shade would conceal him till he could have opportunity to escape unobserved.

"The night, at length, approached, in which he determined to put his plan into execution. But what if he should fail? It might be the last of his earthly existence.

"About dark, the sentinels were stationed, as usual, round the house. They were four in number.

"Before midnight, all was still. Officers and soldiers were asleep. Crosby rose, and holding his chains, so that

they should not clink, crept softly to the window, which he raised. Fast did his heart beat, while doing this. But faster still as he slid to the ground, beneath the willow tree.

"A sentinel was at no great distance. For a moment, he stopped. Arrested by the noise. He even turned. Listened. Looked. But all was now silent there. And thinking himself mistaken, he sung aloud 'All's well,' and onward he marched, still farther from the place of Crosby's concealment.

"Now, thought he, is the moment. The only moment, perhaps, which I shall have. Creeping on his hands and feet, he reached the grave yard, a stone's throw from the church, and here behind a tombstone, succeeded in loosing his chains.

"When this was done, he watched the moment to make his escape. A thick swamp, he knew, was at no great distance. But the darkness of the night made haste dangerous. Yet in rapidity lay his only hope.

"He prepared, therefore, to run the hazard. And seizing the moment, when the sentinel had turned in an opposite direction, he bounded forth and fled. A ball passed him before he had reached many rods. And now another. And still another.

"Yet a merciful providence protected him. And, before the garrison could be roused, he was wallowing deep in the mud of a swamp. But he was safe. Quite safe from pursuers."

Visit To A Cave

G*en. P:* "The escape of Crosby was a hair-breadth one, and well did he know it. He felt himself indeed safe from his pursuers. But his situation was no comfortable one. Up to his knees in mud, and without a shelter for the night.

"He determined, therefore, to grope his way through the swamp. And, if possible, to reach the dwelling of Mr. -. Before morning. This he found a difficult task. Bushes and briers and quagmires impeded his course. And several times he was on the point of giving up the effort, and waiting till day light.

"By slow degrees, however, he went forward. Sometimes, indeed, sinking unexpectedly deep into the mud. Or, when he thought himself firm on a bog. Sliding away, and coming down upon all fours. At length it was his good fortune, to emerge from the thicket, in an hour or so from which, he knocked at the door of the gentleman to whom he had been referred by the committee of safety.

"Mr. -. Had been informed, that he might be expected that night, and was accordingly still up. A good supper was in readiness for him, and heartily did the gentleman congratulate him on his escape.

"When he had finished his meal 'Well,' said the gentleman, 'I have an important message to deliver to you.'

"'What is it?' inquired Crosby.

"'The committee of safety wish you to cross the Hudson immediately, where you are to take measures to seize an English officer, and a company of tories whom he has enlisted on that side.'

"'Cross tonight?' asked Crosby.

"'Immediately,' replied Mr. - 'no time is to be lost. You are fatigued. But once on the other side, you will be more safe, and can take rest.'

"'I will go,' said Crosby.

"'And I will set you across myself,' said the gentleman, 'it is only a short distance.'

"Accordingly they proceeded to the river, where a boat was in readiness, in which they soon reached the opposite shore.

"Having received the necessary directions, Crosby now proceeded on his course. And, by the hour of breakfast, had reached the ground where he was to begin his operations.

"At a farm house, near where he found himself he obtained a comfortable breakfast. After finishing which, he made himself known as a shoemaker, and begged employment.

"'Why,' said the farmer, 'just at present, we are pretty well shod.'

"'Well,' observed Crosby, 'perhaps you have other work, about which you can employ me. I can turn my hand to almost any kind of farming business.'

"'No doubt. No doubt,' said the farmer, 'you are no fool. From Yankee land, I guess. No matter. Well, I don't care if you stay a couple of days, or so, and help me and my wife kill hogs, and a few such notions.'

"Terms were soon settled, and Crosby proved quite knowing and helpful."

While they were dealing with farmer works, a noise was heard. "What noise is that?' asked Crosby, while he was helping, 'Can it be thunder?'

"'More like cannon,' said the farmer 'loud talk below, I rather guess.'

"'Hard times for Washington just now,' observed Crosby, 'and some think pretty justly.'

"'Why,' said the farmer, 'Why. It won't do to speak all one thinks. But. Well. Why don't you turn soldier? You look as though you could fight, upon a pinch?'

"'Well, I think, I might,' said Crosby. 'Have you any place of enlistment hereabouts, that a body could join, if one were so minded?'

"'Why,' replied the farmer, 'I don't know but I could put you in a way, if you are one of the right sort of men.'

"'What sort do you wish?' inquired Crosby.

"'Oh, lower party men. They are more fashionable hereabouts.'

"'Well, I like to be in the fashion, wherever I am,' observed Crosby.

"'Good!' said the farmer, 'do you see yonder mountain, west?'

"'I do,' replied Crosby.

"'Well, if you wish to see as fine a fellow as ever carried sword, there is your man, and right glad would he be of your bone and muscle. Good pay. Light work, I tell you.'

"'Can I be introduced to him?' asked Crosby.

"'That you can. Tonight. I've shown many a lad like yourself the way to make a fortune.'

"In the evening the farmer was as good as his word. Giving Crosby a wink, they went forth, shaping their course towards the mountain, about half way up which, they came to a huge rock, which jutted over with threatening aspect. But it was prevented from falling, by several forest trees, against which it rested."

"Here the farmer, taking his cane, struck several smart blows upon the rock. Instantly, a kind of trap door was opened, and an English captain appeared, with a lantern.

"'Captain!' whispered the farmer, 'here's as brave a lad as you have seen this many a day. Good bye.'

"'Well, my lad,' said the captain, 'do you understand burrowing?'

"'Not much of the wood chuck about me,' replied Crosby, 'more of the fox. I can enter burrows already made.'

"'Well! see whether your skill can contrive to enter here,' pointing to a small hole, leading into a cavern.

"'Tight work, I believe,' said Crosby, forcing his huge frame through the opening, followed by the captain, who, from the smallness of his size, slipped down with more ease.

"'Quite a comfortable apartment, captain,' observed Crosby, casting his eye round upon the interior, 'and not likely to starve very soon, one would judge, from the good things on your table.'

"'Help yourself to what you like,' said the captain, 'his majesty's friends provide well. Good fare. No charges.'

"Crosby had but just supped. But tempted by the fare, somewhat superior to that which he had seen at the farmer's, he seated himself at the table, while the liberal hand of the captain was not backward in replenishing his plate, as often as it was emptied.

"'Do you leave here soon?' inquired Crosby.

"'Tomorrow, I hope,' said the captain. 'I have burrowed here long enough. Much longer. And I shall have claws in good earnest.'

"'Your company is full, then?'

"'Room for one or two more. What say you, shall I enter your name?'

"'When and where does the company meet, before marching?' inquired Crosby.

"'On Tuesday evening, at the barn of Mr. S - . What say you, will you be present?'

"'I will,' replied Crosby.

"'Done!' said the captain 'now turn in. And in the morning, go back to farmer B - 's, and be ready to meet us, at the time and place appointed.'

"On the following morning, which was Saturday, Crosby returned to his employer, with whom he concluded to stay, till the appointed time of marching. "Much now depended on good management. News of the above arrangement must he sent to the committee of safety, and as early as possible.

At some distance from farmer B - 's, Crosby had ascertained there lived an honest old whig, whom he determined to employ to carry a letter to Mr. Jay, then at Fishkill.

"Accordingly, having prepared a letter, he hastened, on the setting in of evening, to fulfil his purpose. In this he succeeded to his wishes. And, before the usual hour of rest, had returned, without exciting the suspicion of any one.

"The important Tuesday evening, at length, arrived, and brought together, at the appointed place, the captain and about thirty tories. Crosby was early on the spot, and before eleven, he was the only individual of the whole class, who was not quietly asleep.

"At length, some one without was heard by him to cough. This being the signal agreed upon, Crosby coughed in return. And the next minute, the barn was filled with a body of captain Townsend's celebrated rangers; 'surrender!' exclaimed Townsend, in a tone, which brought every tory upon his feet 'surrender! or, by the life of Washington, you'll not see day light again.'

"It was in vain to resist, and the English officer delivered up his sword. "'Call your muster-roll,' ordered Capt. Townsend. "The Englishman did as directed. And, at length, came to the name of Enoch Crosby.

"No one answered. Crosby had concealed him self,

with the hope of escaping. But, finding this impossible, he presented himself before Captain Townsend, and Col. Duer, one of the committee of safety, who was present.

"'Ah! is it you, Crosby?' asked Townsend. 'You had light heels at Fishkill. But, my word for it, you will find them heavy enough after this.'

"'Who is he?' inquired Col. Duer, as if he knew him not, though he knew him well, yet not daring to recognize him.

"'Who is he!' exclaimed Townsend, 'Enoch Crosby, sir. Like an eel, slipping out of one's finger's as water runs down hill. But he'll not find it so easy a matter to escape again.'

"The party were soon on their way to Fishkill, where they arrived in the course of an hour or two, and lodged their prisoners in the old Dutch church.

"Crosby was not thus fortunate. Townsend's quarters were at some distance, and to these Crosby was quite civilly invited to go. As the captain declared, he wished to have him under his own eye.

"On his arrival, Crosby was placed in a room by himself. He was heavily ironed, and a trusty guard detached to see that he came to 'no harm,' as the captain said.

"During the expedition, which had occupied some twelve or fourteen hours, the company had fasted. Supper was therefore prepared with some haste, after the return of the officer, who, on sitting down, fairly gorged himself with food and wine.

"About midnight Crosby was unexpectedly awakened, by a gentle shake. On opening his eyes, whom should he see before him but a female, who assisted in doing the work of the family.

'Here, Enoch Crosby.' said she, 'rise and follow me, say nothing. Hold fast your chains."

"Crosby was not at first satisfied, whether it were a dream or a reality. But quite willing to make his escape, he rose as he was bid, and followed her.

"As they passed from the room, there lay the sentinel, extended at full length, dreaming of battles, it might be. But certainly, very quiet as to the safety of his prisoner.

"'Some virtue in Miller's opiates,' whispered the girl. "'That's the secret, is it?' asked Crosby, in rather a louder tone than was pleasant to his attendant.

"'Hush! hush!' said she, 'or the Philistines will be upon you.'"

Henry: "Pray, father, what did she mean by Miller's opiates?"

Gen. P: "Miller was a physician in those parts, and kept an apothecary's store. By some means, the girl had obtained from him anodyne or sleeping potions, which she had put into the food, or drink, of both the captain and his sentinels. 'They sleep well,' said Crosby, on descending from the chamber to the first floor, where he could hear the loud breathing of the captain.

"'I hope they'll sleep till morning,' rejoined the girl. 'Stay! a moment, till I put the key of your door into the captain's pocket.' "'What?' asked Crosby, 'does he keep the key himself?' "'Yes, indeed,' replied the girl. 'He was determined that you should play no more yankee tricks, as he said, while under his care.'

"'He must have thought me a man of some contrivance, to take such precaution.'

"'Oh!' said the girl, 'I've often heard him call you the. A bad name. At least, he said he believed that you and the old boy understood one another pretty well.'

"'I wonder what he'll think now?' said Crosby.

"The key being once more safely in the pocket of the Captain, the girl conducted Crosby out of the door, and pointing towards a mountain lying to the west, now but just discernible. "'Hasten thither,' said she, 'and lie concealed till the coming search is over.'

"'But tell me,' said Crosby, 'before I go, how will you escape suspicion?'

"'Oh!' said the girl, laughing, 'never fear for me. I shall be out of harm's way before morning.'

"'One more question,' said Crosby 'who put it into your heart to deliver me?'

"'Jay is your friend,' said she,. Waving her head 'farewell.' "To Crosby, the whole was now plain. With a light heart, he directed his course towards the mountain pointed out. And before morning, he was safely hid in some of its secret recesses.

"Capt. Townsend awoke at his usual hour, having slept away the anodyne potion which had been administered to him.

"The key to Crosby's door was still in his pocket. And

not a suspicion had ever entered his mind, that Crosby himself was not safely in his room.

“The hour at length coming, when Crosby’s meal was to be given, Townsend himself opened the door. He started back, on looking in, and seeing no one.

“‘What!’ exclaimed he, ‘empty!. Impossible!. Here!’ vociferated he, in a tone of thunder.’Sentinel, what is the meaning of all this?’

But no one could tell. No noise had been heard. The shutters of the room were safely closed. The door was locked. The key was in his pocket.

“Due search was now made. Every nook and corner were examined. But not a trace of the vagrant was discovered.

“‘Well!’ said the captain, ‘I thought Crosby and the -. , were in league. Now I know it.’“

The Adventures Of Crosby

G*en. P:* "Crosby, as I said, was in a safe retreat, on the mountain, before morning." *William:* "Were any measures adopted to retake him?"

Gen. P: "No very active measures, probably. But Townsend declared, that if Crosby should ever fall in his way again, he would give him a halter forthwith.

"During the following night, our hero descended the mountain, in a southerly direction. And at a late breakfast hour, the next morning, came to a farm house, the kind mistress of which gave him a comfortable meal.

"For several days from this time, Crosby wandered round the country, without any certain object. He greatly wished for an interview with the Committee of Safety. But the attempt he found would be hazardous. Until the troops in the immediate neighbourhood of Fishkill, it should be sent on some expedition, at a distance.

"This was a gloomy period for Crosby. Although conscious of toiling in a good cause, and of promoting the interests of his country. Somehow, he felt alone. Not a friend had he to whom he could unbosom his cares. And often was he houseless, and in want.

"Besides, he began to be known. To be suspected. And the double and treble caution, which he found it necessary to exercise, made his employment almost a burden.

"While maturing some plan, by which he could effect an interview with the Committee of Safety, he called, just at evening, at a farm house, and requested a night's lodging. This was readily granted him, and he laid aside his pack, thankful to find a resting place, after the toils of the day.

"It was not long, before two very large men, armed with muskets, entered the house. One of them started on seeing Crosby, and whispered something to his companion, to which the latter apparently assented.

"Then, turning to Crosby 'I have seen you before, I think, sir?' said he.

"'Probably,' replied Crosby, 'though I cannot say that I recollect you.'

"'Perhaps not. But I am sure you were not long since at Fishkill? ha?'"

"'The very fellow!' exclaimed the other 'you recollect how he escaped. Seize him!'

"In a moment, the strong hand of the first was laid upon him, and his grasp was the grasp of an Anakim. And though Crosby might have been a match for him alone,. Prudence forbade resistance. They were two. He was but one. They were armed with muskets. He had no weapon about him.

"'Tomorrow,' said the principal, 'you shall go to head quarters, where, my word for it, you'll swing without much ceremony. The committee will never take the trouble to try you again, and Townsend declares that he wishes only to come once more within gun shot of you.'

"'Is it so?' asked Crosby.

"'Even so'. Replied the stranger 'your time is short.'

"Crosby was seldom alarmed. But now he could perceive real danger. Could he be fairly tried he might escape. But to be delivered into Townsend's hands, and perhaps the Committee of Safety at a distance. He might, indeed, come to harm.

"He had one resort. He could show his pass, and it might save him. Accordingly, drawing it forth, he presented it to his captors; 'Read that,' said he, 'and then say, whether I am worthy of death.'

"Astonishment sat on the countenances of both while they read the pass. When it was finished, the principal observed, 'I am satisfied. We have been deceived. Others are deceived also. You are at liberty to go where you please. This is the hand-writing of Mr. Jay. I know it well.'

"Crosby might, perhaps, have staid where he was through the night. But his feelings were such, that he preferred to seek other lodgings. Accordingly, shouldering his pack, he set forth in quest of a resting place. Which at the distance of a couple of miles, he was so fortunate as to obtain.

"But he was destined to other troubles. Scarcely had he laid aside his pack, and taken a seat near a comfortable fire, before a man entered, whom he was sure that he had seen before.

"At the same time, the stranger cast upon him an eye of deep scrutiny, and increasing severity.

"'A cool evening abroad'. Observed Crosby.

"The stranger made no reply. But springing upon his feet, darted upon him, like a fiend.

"'Now, I know you'. Exclaimed he 'I thought it was you. You are the villain who betrayed us to the Committee of Safety. Clear out from the house quickly, or I'll call one of my neighbours, who says that if he ever sees you again, he'll suck your very heart's blood.'

"'Ah!' said Crosby, quite calm and collected 'perhaps'

"'Leave this house instantly'. Vociferated the man, now nearly choked with rage 'but before you go, take one pounding.'

"'A pounding!' exclaimed Crosby, in contempt 'Come then,'. Rising like a lion from his lair 'Come,'. Said he, at the same time rolling up his sleeves, and showing a pair of fists, which resembled a trip-hammer for hardness.

"'Come on, and I'll try you a pull'. The muscles of his arm contracting, and lying out like cart-ropes the whole length. From shoulder to wrist. And his countenance, at the same time, looking as terrific as a madman's 'Come on,' said he."

"'Why! we-we-ll. Upon the whole'. Said the man 'I. I. Think I'll let you off, if you'll never set foot here again.'

"'I'll promise no such thing,' said Crosby. 'I'm willing to go. Indeed, I would, not stay in such a habitation as this. But I'll not be driven.'

"Crosby well knew that prudence required his departure. And with some deliberation, he shouldered his pack once more, and with a short 'good by', left the house. At the distance of a mile, he found lodgings where he slept unmolested.

"On the following morning, he ascertained that the Committee of Safety were alone at Fishkill. The troops having gone abroad on some expedition. Seizing the opportunity of their absence, he crossed the river, and was soon at the residence of Mr. Duer.

"That Crosby was in more than ordinary danger in traversing the country, was apparent both to himself and Mr. Duer. He was advised, therefore, to repair to an honest old Dutchman's, who lived in a retired place, some miles distant, and there wait until farther orders.

"Accordingly, being furnished with a complete set of tools, he proceeded to the appointed place, and was so fortunate as to find ample employ for some time, under the very roof of his host.

"A few days only, however, had elapsed, when an express arrived, bringing him a letter from Mr. Duer.

"The worthy old Dutchman was quite curious to know from whom the letter came, and what was its purport.

"'Val,' said he, knocking the ashes from his pipe 'you know tee shentlemen of tee armee? Vat for tey rite you? Eh?'

"Crosby waived an answer as well as he was able, informing his host that he must be absent a short time, when he would return, and finish the shoes.

"'Val,' said the Dutchman, 'how you go?. On shank's mare? You no trudge so. You nebber get tere. Here, you Hauns! Puckle tee pest shaddle on mine horse, and pring him to tee horse plock tirectly. You hear?'

"The horse was brought out accordingly, and Crosby was soon on his way to Fishkill. On his arrival, circumstances existed, which rendered it imprudent for him to tarry, and he was directed to go to Dr. Miller's, who kept an apothecary's shop at some distance, and there wait the arrival of one of the Committee of Safety.

"On reaching the place, he inquired for Dr. Miller, who he was told was absent. This information was given him by a girl, whom he was sure he had seen before, but where he could not recollect.

"'If you wish to trade,' said the girl, "I can wait upon you. Perhaps you would like some of Dr. Miller's opiates. You recollect they are quite powerful."

"Crosby was on the point of exclaiming. But the girl whispered him to be silent. 'These men,' said she, 'who are around us, are whigs. But you must not let your name be known.'

"While thus conversing, and listening to the conversation of several men, at the fire, a stranger entered the shop, and inquired for a vial of medicine. Crosby recognized that it was Mr. Jay. So slipping out of the door, he pretended to be admiring the stranger's fine horse, when Mr. Jay came out. And, as he mounted, whispered to Crosby to return to the Dutchman's, and wait for farther orders.

"Accordingly, he soon after left Miller's, and before night was again at his quarters.

"'Sho, ten, you cot pack'. Said the Dutchman as Crosby rode into the yard. The smoke at the same time running in a fine curl from his mouth.

'Safe home again,' replied Crosby.

"'Yaw, tee horse pe true. True. He vill ride any potty rite to mine ouse. Hauns! here. Take off his shaddle. Rup him toun mit a whisp of shtraw. Tont let him trink till he coutch'd cuoold.'

"A few days from this time, Crosby received definite instructions from the Committee of Safety, to repair to Vermont, on a secret expedition. And as no time was to be lost, he was obliged to bid his Dutchman host adieu, quite suddenly.

"'Can you direct me the road to S.,' asked Crosby.

"'To S.? Do you see that road upon the hel?'

"'O, yes,' said Crosby, 'I see it."'

"'Val, you musht not take dat roat. But, I tell you vat, you musht go right straight by the parn, and vere you see yon roat dat crooks just so. See here'. Bending his elbow 'you must go right strait. Ten you vill turn de potato patch round, de pridge over, and de river up stream, and de hel up. And tirectly you see mine prother Haunse's parn shingled mit straw. Dat's his house, vare mine prother Schnven lives. He'll tell you so petter as I can. And you go little farther, you see two roats. You musht not take bote of 'em. Understand?'

"'Quite plain! quite plain!' said Crosby. Adding in a low tone to himself, 'that you are a Dutchman. Well, friend, good morning."'

His Northern Tour

"We shall not attempt to follow Crosby on his northern tour. Nor to relate the many adventures with which he met during his absence. He proved of great service to the cause of his country. But often suffered much by being taken with tories, whose capture he was instrumental in effecting.

"At length he returned to the theatre of his former operations. But he was now suspected by the tories of being a secret friend to the whigs, and opposed to the royal cause.

"He was, therefore, narrowly watched, and even found it necessary to hide himself at a brother-in-law's in the Highlands. Nor was he even here secure, for on the second night after reaching his brother-in-law's residence, a musket was discharged through the window at him, the ball of which grazed his neck, and tore the collar of his coat.

"It was apparent from this circumstance that his retreat was known. But it was rendered quite certain a few nights after, by the appearance of an armed gang at the door, who having burst in, dragged Crosby's brother-in-law from the bed, and demanded where Crosby slept.

"This information, for a time, was refused. But at length, death was threatened, in case of refusal, and his bed chamber was pointed out.

"Crosby heard the coming of the assailants, and sprung to his gun. But, before he could reach it, a ruffian had snapped a pistol at his head. Fortunately, it missed fire. But now a most desperate engagement followed, in which Crosby showed the most astonishing strength and agility. But numbers, at length, overpowered him, and he was left for dead.

"Life, however, was not extinct. And after the ruffians had retired, Crosby in a measure came to himself. But months passed away before he was able to resume the business, in which he had been engaged. Indeed, after this period, less was required. The long and bloody contest was in a measure drawing to a close. Liberty, for which so many had fought and bled, was destined to take up her delightful abode on the American soil.

"But had the same necessity existed, it was apparent that Crosby must be released. It was becoming dangerous for him to be seen abroad. He was known to many, to whose capture he had been directly instrumental. Such were of course bitter against him, and needed only an opportunity to wreak their vengeance upon him. Yet he continued with the army some time longer. At length his time of service expired, upon which he returned to South-East, where he still lives."

William: "What! alive yet, father?"

Gen. P: "Yes, still living, and enjoying the pleasant reflection that millions are freemen, whom he helped to make free. But who, without his labours, and those of kindred spirits, might this day be doing homage to British power."

Activities

Match A and B

A

- But I do not know more than that
- The neighbours would sometimes happen
- When Enoch was, sixteen years of age,
- Besides, they saw no reason.
- And, besides, living in the country, and being acquainted
- Young, who lived at a distance, in a direction
- He had a strong wish to join the army, and

B

- misfortune came upon his father.
- with it, they could do even more injury than strangers.
- somewhat different from that which he was taking.
- why they should be slaves
- in there of a winter's evening to spend an hour.
- they are a kind of shot."
- believed that he should go along.

Choose and Fill

- P: "Do_?_wish_?_know the_?_meaning of_?_words, my son? (you / the / original / to)
- "Those_?_used_?_to be_?_over, at_?_Mr.

  (things / old / talked / often)
- It was_?_as_?_told you,_?_those who_?_for the liberty of America." (applied, / fought / to / I)
- The officers_?_them_?_rally, to_?_their ground,_?_ they did so. (called / and / stand / to)
- "During_?_labours_?_the Americans,_?_enemy continued_?_annoy them, by throwing shells from the fort." (these / to / the / of)
- *William:*_?_evening_?_British soldiers_?_near a_?_in Boston. ("One / ropewalk / were / some)
- or sat_?_to_?_customer of_?_master, who_?_in, on a rainy day. (listening / happened / his / some)
- Hutchinson had_?_come_?_and told_?_people.

  (not / the / out,)
- It then_?_and_?_scattering fragments_?_iron often_?_ horrible execution." (bursts, / do / of / the)
- Within a_?_hours,_?_people had_?_

  (few / assembled. / many)
- This they_?_manfully,_?_though some_?_the others_?_the more determined.

  (met / seemed / fell, / and,)
- I_?_think_?_knew enough,_?_to ask_?_foolish a question." (should / so / not / you)

- P: “No,_?_he_?_asked to_?_introduced to_?_of the tories.” (no, / some / be / only)
- He had_?_hard_?_in the_?_campaign, and_?_rest.

  (seen / needed / northern / service,)
- ‘ Crosby_?_up,_?_directly over_?_a shell_?_descending.” (looked / was / him, / and)
- And he_?_to_?_it said,_?_he could_?_make sacrifices. (scorned / not / that / have)
- Many arguments_?_support_?_way of_?_and strongly_?_they urge Crosby to go with them.

  (to / did / thinking, / their)
- ‘But,’ said_?_as_?_shook hands_?_the unsuspicious _?_and bade him farewell, ‘I shall doubtless have the pleasure of seeing .“(he, / farmer, / with / he)
- And when_?_had_?_’Are you_?_asked the_?_’to accompany a body of horse to the spot, and attempt to (he / committee, / willing,’ / finished,)
- “‘You_?_have_?_opportunity,’ said_?_committee.

  (shall / the / an)
- In the_?_time,_?_company had_?_and now,_?_the darkness of the night, were arranging their plans - “

  (mean / amid / assembled, / the)
- ‘You shall_?_them_?_said the_?_’it would_?_well to meet. (see / be / captain, / together,’)
- But to_?_down_?_see them_?_arms.

  (march / ground / and)

Put the words in the sentence order.

- P:/so/spy/a/"Well,/real/is/generally/considered./
- Two/through/Mill/Croton/called/rivers,/the/and/the/river,/ wind/place./the/
- trade./to/and/loved/"Enoch/labour,/was/willing/learn/a/
- He/solid,/wax,/with/assigned/a/had/seat/him/provided/ awls,/more/thread,/the/and/but/equally/needful/ companion,/lapstone./a/
- It/shop./in/sit/tiresome/was/to/all/day,/a/confined/
- He/man./a/was/grave/
- A/not/them/said/in/who/man,/worked/the/ropewalk,/ something/did/to/they/which/like,/and/they/beat/him./
- The/the/parliament/British/taxed/Americans./
- man?/Crosby/"Was/*John:*/Enoch/a/minute/
- out,/before/nearly/of/the/"On/5th/March,/1770/a/was/ year/ time/Enoch's/the/'Boston/Massacre'/happened."/
- The/which/called/the/part/lower/of/mortar/is/the/ powder./ chamber,/the/contains/
- read/"I/*William:*/have/about/it./
- P:/son./are/well/it/"Tell/as/as/you/able,/my/
- In/again./join/he/few/a/days,/resolved/to/the/army/
- or/Crosby,/man/in/was/"It/not/such/a/as/ease,/Enoch/ seek/ to/shun/danger,/in/the/of/hour/trial./his/country's/
- And/well/not/that/have/scorned/he/to/it/said,/he/as/ could/ sacrifices,/make/as/others./

- the/of/latter/party'/the/Americans/'upper/because/the/lay/ north/former./the/
- oneself,/say/stranger,/observed/"'Why,'/the/'one/ mus'n't/ much/days./about/these/in/
- many/to/did/thinking,/their/to/arguments/support/way/ of/ and/Crosby/strongly/urge/they/go/with/them./
- his/now/beyond/was/"He/soon/harm,/and/travelled/at/ ease./
- The/of/the/Crosby's/fell/light/on/face,/and/searching/ eye/ Mr./
- the/'come/than/conviction/face/of/expression/Crosby's/ carrying/more/of/do/honesty,/could/words/in./
- Young/neighbouring/retired/Crosby/and/now/to/a/inn./
- mounted,/of/time,/the/"'At/appointed/a/company/troop/Pla-ins./well/White/left/
- Congress'./of/in/demand/"'We/it/the/name/the/ Continental/
- you?/the/to/are/"'You/going/enlist/into/army,/are/
- His/at/country,/go/was/design/to/round/the/and/work/ tra-de./his/
- perhaps,/to/work/have/you/some/for/me/do?/
- see/Crosby/"Why/*Henry:*/did/wish/to/that?/
- But/what/enough/hadn't/he/brains/to/think/was/inside./
- day/his/apparently/Crosby/"While/was/making/up/ mind,/ the/by./passed/
- urged/he/of/the/"In/course/the/day,/was/strongly/enlist./to/
- It/among/of/a/was/season/great/joy/them./

Answer the wh questions

- When would his father wish to have his son soldier?
- Which subjects were discussed when as he grew older and was at home occasionally, on a visit?
- Where was soon roused?
- What also produced resolution?
- Whose musket was taken down, and fitting on the knap-sack?
- Who fell in with a stranger, who appeared to be pas-sing in the same direction with?
- Why did the committee of safety consisted of men of distinction friendly?
- When will they help to escape?

WWS

Who said?

William; Crosby; John; The farmer; Mr. Jay; Henry ; The general ; Mr. Crosby; Capt. Benedict;

What said?

- "The time will come, when the people will defend them-selves."
- "Father! William says you are going to tell us a story about the war!"
- "Your resolution is honourable"
- "Did the captain show him the roll?"
- "'What! Have you got back, Crosby?"
- "Did the people find walnuts there, father?"
- "It is monstrous."
- "True, I will accompany you. "
- "I must tell you one story more."

Dictionary

accordingly	göre
advice	tavsiye
aloud	yüksek sesle
anodyne	yatıştırıcı
appear	görünür
ascertain	anlamak
assent	kabullenmek
attempt	girişim
back	geri
bayonet	süngü
believe	inanmak
beneath	altında
bible	incil
blows	darbeler
born	doğmuş
brightening	parlatma
brotherinlaws	*üvey kardeş*
bursts	patlamalar
cares	umurunda
cause	neden
ceremony	tören
charges	ücretler
companies	firmalar
concerted	toplu
confusion	karışıklık
contain	içeren
contracting	sözleşme
corner	köşe
couple	çift
deep	derin
delivered	teslim
descending	azalan
dismay	dehşet
drop	düşmek
duty	görev
elapsed	geçen
employed	istihdam
employer	işveren
enemy	düşman
enlisted	kaydolmak
enterprise	kurumsal
evening	akşam
exciting	heyecan verici
faintness	zayıflık
fancy	fantezi
farewell	veda
fashionable	moda
fastened	tutturulmuş
feeble	zayıf
flight	uçuş
garret	tavan arası
gentleman	beyefendi
gloomy	kasvetli
gradually	kademeli olarak
grope	okşamak
gun	*silah*
hardship	sıkıntı
hark	kulak vermek
haughty	mağrur
head	kafa
headlong	paldır küldür
hearts	kalpler
hence	bundan dolayı
hit	saklamak
honest	dürüst
horsemen	atlı
instantly	anında
idleness	aylaklık
inches	inç
indeed	gerçekten
information	bilgi
injure	yaralamak
insulte	hakaret
intention	niyet
interrupt	kesmek
jutt	uzanmak
keep	tutmak
kitchen	mutfak
knees	dizler
labour	emek
lane	şerit
lead	kurşun
league	lig
leave	ayrılmak
length	uzunluk
lights	ışıklar
likely	muhtemelen
lodged	teslim
lost	kayıp
lump	topak
manner	şekilde
martyr	şehit
master	usta
meadow	çayır

meeting	toplantı
memory	hafıza
merciful	merhametli
military	askeri
miller	değirmenci
ministers	bakanlar
monstrous	korkunç
mortars	harçları
muscle	kas
narrowly	dar
neck	boyun
noise	gürültü
northern	kuzey
notions	kavramlar
object	nesne
occasion	fırsat
occupied	meşgul
onward	ileriye
oppress	ezmek
oppressive	baskıcı
others	diğerleri
otherwise	aksi
overtake	sollamak
overwhelmed	boğulmuş
own	kendi
pairs	çiftler
parents	ebeveyn
party	parti
patch	yama
pay	ödeme
peal	gürlemek
permission	izin
persuaded	ikna
physician	hekim
pilotage	pilotaj
pipe	boru
places	yerler
plung	dalmak
pointing	işaretleme
potions	iksirler
powder	toz
pray	dua
premises	tesislerinde
prevent	engellemek
proceed	devam etmek
properly	düzgün
providence	ihtiyat
pursue	sürdürmek
reach	ulaşmak
reality	gerçeklik
recognize	tanımak
refuse	ret etmek
require	gerekli
ride	binmek
rolling	yuvarlanma
runs	ishal
safely	güvenli
sailed	yelken
savages	vahşiler
say	demek
school	okul
seat	oturmak
setting	ayarı
shop	mağaza
showing	gösterme
shout	*bağırmak*
slaughter	katletmek
slipping	kayma
tears	gözyaşı
terms	terimler
threatening	tehdit
thus	böylece
tour	tur
travel	seyahat
trial	deneme
true	gerçek
tune	melodi
uncharged	doldurulmamış
unsatisfactory	yetersiz
use	kullanım
valiant	yiğit
vat	fıçı
villain	kötü adam
wander	gezinmek
watch	izlemek
weakness	güçsüzlük
weariness	yorgunluk
weve	kapılmak
whom	kime
whose	kimin
willing	istekli
wood	ahşap
worst	en kötü
worry	*merak etmek*
yaw	rotadan çıkmak